Who's a Clever Girl, Then?

Jake Juggins and his pirate band decide they need a girl on board ship to do the chores while they get on with having adventures. But the little girl they choose to do their cleaning, cooking and sewing has other ideas.

The Not-So-Clever Genie

Not long after her adventure with the pirates, Mary Mansfield finds a dusty old bottle with a genie inside. The genie grants her three wishes and Mary has lots of ideas about how to use them. Unfortunately the genie has some strong opinions of his own about the kind of wishes suitable for a little girl!

You Herman, Me Mary

When Mary Mansfield sees a big strong man swinging through the trees she knows she's in for another adventure. He may be the new King of the Jungle but he can't read, so it's a good job Mary is there to help out when Wanda goes missing.

Who's a Clever Girl, Then?

Who's a Clever

Rose Impey

ILLUSTRATIONS
André Amstutz

Girl, Then? and other stories

Who's a Clever Girl, Then?
The Not-So-Clever Genie
You Herman, Me Mary

MAMMOTH

First published in Great Britain as three separate
volumes:

Who's a Clever Girl, Then?
published 1985 by William Heinemann Ltd
Text copyright © Rose Impey 1985

The Not-So-Clever Genie
published 1987 by William Heinemann Ltd
Text copyright © Rose Impey 1987

You Herman, Me Mary
published 1989 by William Heinemann Ltd
Text copyright © Rose Impey 1989

This edition first published 1993 by Mammoth
an imprint of Reed Consumer Books Limited
Michelin House, 81 Fulham Road, London SW3 6RB
and Auckland, Melbourne, Singapore and Toronto

Reprinted 1993

This edition text copyright © Rose Impey 1993
Illustrations copyright © André Amstutz 1993

ISBN 0 7497 1530 8

A CIP catalogue record for this title
is available from the British Library

Printed and bound in Great Britain
by Cox & Wyman Ltd, Reading, Berkshire

Contents

Who's a Clever Girl, Then?

1 The Pirate Gang

If you think this is the kind of story where five children, armed only with a bucket and spade, catch a dangerous band of smugglers, you'd be wrong. And if you think this is the kind of story where a poor, helpless little girl is captured by a terrible gang of cut-throat pirates . . . you'd still be wrong, but a lot closer. Now, those are all the hints I'm going to give you. To find out what happens, you'd better read on . . .

Once upon a time, and not so very long ago, a little girl was walking to school. She was a sensible sort of girl, who could make her own packed lunch and do her mum's shopping without losing the change. She was also far too sensible to talk to strange men whom she met in the street, especially ones with peg-legs, scars

9

on their faces, patches over their eyes and scruffy parrots on their shoulders. So when she saw four strange characters fitting this description, she quickly turned the other way and kept on walking.

But the pirates had seen *her*. She was just what they were looking for.

'You look a sensible little girl,' growled the biggest pirate, who was called Jake. 'We want a sensible little girl like you to join our gang, don't we, lads?'

'Yes, yes,' agreed the rest of the gang, covering their mouths to hide their smiles.

'We're rough, tough pirates and we sail the seas in a mighty, fine pirate ship. We have rare adventures, don't we, lads?' boasted Jake.

'Oh yeah, yeah,' said the rest of the gang. They didn't seem quite so sure about this.

'All we need is for you to join us, then we can go off on raids. Isn't that right, lads?' said Jake.

'Yes! Yes!' they agreed, more strongly this time, again covering their mouths to hide their smiles.

Now the little girl knew better than to listen to this kind of story from such wicked-looking villains. She knew they were up to no good. But the idea of having an adventure was far too tempting to miss. She didn't exactly stop, but she walked on more slowly.

'Come on, what do you say? Good Gravy! It would be more fun than going to school, I'll be bound,' said Jake.

Well, the little girl couldn't argue with that, could she?

She stopped and stared into Jake's big, black eyes.

'Would you really make me into a proper pirate?'

'On my honour,' swore Jake, trying hard to look honest.

'Would you give me a proper pirate outfit?'

'To be sure, my hearty,' said Jake.

The other pirates stepped forward and gave her a scarf and a hat and a belt and a patch.

'What about a parrot?' she said.

For a moment Jake was put out, but he settled the parrot on the little girl's shoulder.

'Grilled Gammon! You strike a hard bargain,' he snarled. 'Now, let's be off. Back to the ship.'

The little girl was pleased with herself. The pirates looked happy too. They thought they had tricked her 'good and proper'. And, if you don't tell the little girl, I'll tell you why.

You see, these pirates were not too happy. They used to sail the seas in a battered ship called *The Leaky Tub*. And it did leak too. The pirates didn't mind, as long as it stayed afloat. Most of the time it did. Then one day they had a piece of luck. They attacked a handsome galleon. The crew just ran away and, what's more, they never came back. Jake and his men found themselves the proud owners of *The*

Flying Dragon. That was when their problems started.

This ship proved to be a lot of work. It was smart and shiny and it seemed a shame not to keep it clean. Jethro began to scrub and swill the decks. He shone the brass until he could see his face in it. The other pirates liked to see the ship sparkling. It made them feel proud.

There was a cook's galley, with pots and pans and kitchen tools. Joshua liked cooking. He made marvellous meals like seafood risotto, octopus in red wine and chilli sauce, prawn pancakes and 'The Flying Dragon', a wonderful ice-cream dish with peaches and grapes and chocolate sauce.

There was also a cabin full of canvas and sailcloth and needles and thread. Jem was clever at sewing. He could patch the sails and tack and turn a seam. He made curtains and cushions and soon the pirates had new outfits. They enjoyed looking smart.

Finally, there was a cosy captain's cabin, with maps and charts. Jake loved to sit in the captain's chair, with his foot up, planning and plotting routes and dreaming about finding buried treasure.

For a while the pirates were happy but soon Jake wanted some adventure. However, the others were always too busy, cleaning and cooking and mending.

'Jumping Jelly!' Jake roared. 'You're turning into a bunch of ship-wives. This isn't a rest-home for worn out sailors. We're rough, tough pirates. We should be raiding and rampaging.'

The pirates looked ashamed of themselves. But then they said:

'Who's going to cook the meals?'

'Who's going to keep the decks clean?'

'Who will do the making and mending?'

'Giant Jam Tarts! That's girl's work,' snarled Jake. 'We'll get some gullible little girl to do those jobs, then we can have adventures.'

And that is just what they did, as easy as that. Or so they thought, for they were old-fashioned pirates. They didn't realise that little girls are too clever to be caught that way. But don't worry, they're going to find out!

2 The Pirates Find Out

So off they all went, down the road, through the alley, along the path and onto the canal bank. This path ran along the bottom of the school playing-field. The pirates kept their heads down, but the little girl didn't. She would have loved her friends to see her, all dressed up. The pirates couldn't believe how smoothly it had all gone. They thought to themselves, 'Are little girls really that easy to fool?'

When they reached the ship, Jake led the way up the gang-plank.

'Welcome aboard *The Flying Dragon*,' he said. The little girl was amazed by what she saw. Each of the pirates was impatient to show her what work she would have to do. The little girl was surprised to be so popular.

'Those pirates are up to something,' she thought.

15

First, Jethro showed her the decks and cabins. He showed her the mops and buckets and the polish. He told her all she had to do.

'You'd better make a good job of it. I like to see my face in this brass.'

The little girl was surprised. 'I'm not doing the cleaning,' she thought. 'Whoever heard of pirates dusting and polishing?'

Next, Joshua took her to see the cook's galley and showed her the pots and pans.

'We expect good food,' he warned her. 'No lumps in the potatoes, no soggy cabbage, no packet soup.'

The little girl was even more surprised. 'I'm not doing the cooking,' she thought. 'Whoever heard of pirates baking?'

Then Jem showed her the tailor's cabin. He showed her the needles and thread and rolls of material.

'We like to look smart. We can't have holes in our clothes when we go off on raids,' he said.

The little girl began to look cross. 'I'm not doing the mending,' she thought. 'Whoever heard of pirates sewing?'

She was looking for adventure, and she was determined to find it.

At last Jake showed her the captain's cabin. He showed her all his maps and charts. The little girl's eyes widened. Her fingers began to itch.

'Curdled Custard! Keep your female fingers off those charts!' he shouted. 'You can come in here to flick a duster around, if you're careful, but don't touch anything. Plotting and planning is my job and you'd better keep out of my way.'

Now the little girl was mad. She stared into Jake's big, black eyes.

'Did you really think I was going to join a pirate gang to do the cooking and cleaning? Did you think I would fall for a trick like that? Girls don't have to do that kind of thing. Girls can have adventures just like boys because they're just as clever as boys.' And to prove it she came up with a clever plan.

The pirates were surprised and disappointed. If girls didn't do this kind of thing who was going to cook and clean and mend? It seemed they still had their problem after all. The little girl looked at their puzzled faces.

'Don't worry, I know how we can sort this out. We can all have a vote. That way we all decide who should do each job,' she said.

The pirates were completely confused. They had never come across this idea before. She tried to explain. 'We vote for who is the best person for each job. Then, at the end, everyone is happy.

'First,' said the little girl, in her teacher's voice, 'who makes delicious doughnuts, tasty tarts and perfect puddings? Who should do the cooking?'

The pirates began to feel hungry. They all turned to Joshua and pointed at him.

'Good,' said the little girl. 'Then that's decided and *everyone* is happy.'

Joshua didn't look happy, he looked puzzled, but all the others were smiling. They didn't have to do the cooking.

'Now,' said the little girl, 'who can make the brass brightest and the decks dazzle? Who should do the cleaning?'

The pirates liked their smart ship. They all turned to Jethro and pointed at him.

'Good,' said the little girl, 'then that's decided and *everyone* is happy.'

Jethro didn't look happy, he looked puzzled, but all the others were smiling. They didn't have to do the cleaning.

'Next,' said the little girl, 'who can stitch a straight seam and patch a pair of pants? Who should do the sewing?'

The pirates were proud of their fine clothes. They all turned to Jem and pointed at him.

'Good,' said the little girl, 'then that's decided and *everyone* is happy.'

Jem didn't look happy, he looked puzzled, but all the others were smiling. They didn't have to do the sewing.

'Finally,' said the little girl, 'we must choose the captain. This is an important job.'

Jake was smiling. He liked being captain and giving orders. He enjoyed having plenty of time to plot and plan and dream about buried treasure.

But the little girl went on, 'Who is the cleverest person on this ship? Who is best at telling other people what to do? Who is crafty and cunning and good at getting their own way? Who should be captain?'

All the others turned to Jake. He was certainly good at getting his own way. Then they looked at the little girl. She was far more clever and cunning than Jake. They all pointed at her.

'Good,' said the little girl, 'then that's decided and *everyone* is happy. You can be captain's mate,' she said to Jake.

Jake wasn't happy, he was hopping mad, but what could he do?

'Now back to work you good-for-nothing layabouts,' she shouted, 'and be sharp about it.'

The pirates disappeared and soon the ship began to move. *The Flying Dragon* glided along the canal bank until it came to a fork where it joined the wide river. Gathering speed, it sailed down the river until, as the sun was setting, it reached the open sea.

The little girl sat in the captain's chair with her feet on the captain's table. She couldn't believe how smoothly it had gone.

'Are pirates really that easy to fool?' she wondered.

3 Adventures at Sea

Soon the little girl and Jake were busy planning raids. They made attacks on other ships, when they could tempt the pirates away from their cooking and cleaning. They scaled the rigging. They manned the cannons. They hoisted the sails and went in search of adventure.

Their first victory was over a tough sea-dog called Captain Crackers. Some people said he was 105 years old. You would never have guessed it to see him swing from the rigging with a knife between his teeth. But after he met the little girl he decided to retire.

Next, they got the better of a well-known villain, Captain Cut-throat.

'I'll slice you up and feed you to the sharks,' he said. But things didn't work out like that. He was made to walk the plank, along with the rest of his crew.

Their greatest adventure was when they were attacked by a hard-hearted pirate called Captain Bonnet. He and his scurvy crew came aboard *The Flying Dragon* with pistols at the ready, but the ship seemed to be deserted. Jake and his men were hiding. They often did this when the fighting got too fierce. The little girl had climbed the tallest mast. She cut free a huge sail which fell to the deck, trapping the pirates underneath.

Now Jake and the pirates could see what little girls were made of.

After a while the pirates needed a rest. They wanted to get the place ship-shape again. But the little girl had a real taste for adventure now. She was preparing a new plan, to make a pirate raid on her school.

She would terrify the teachers and scare the secretary. She would capture the caretaker and chase the children round the playground. She would take the school by storm and force the headmistress to walk the climbing-frame! She was very excited about this plan.

But the other pirates were not too happy about it.

'Whoever heard of pirates attacking a school full of kids,' grumbled Jake, who was getting fed up with the little girl and her clever ideas.

'That's why it's such a good idea,' said the little girl, 'because nobody would expect it. The element of surprise.'

'But there would be nothing to steal. Who wants hundreds of rulers and pairs of rusty scissors?' said Jethro.

'Ah, but on Mondays there's lots of money. It takes the secretary all morning to count it. I've seen her. Piles of it all over her table.'

The little girl wasn't really interested in the money, it was glory she wanted, but she had to keep the pirates happy.

'There's only five of us. There must be hundreds of them,' said Joshua.

'They don't count,' said the little girl, who felt like a real pirate by now. 'They're just a bunch of kids and a few teachers. They'd be no problem.'

None of the pirates looked convinced. They thought it was a daft idea. The little girl could see she had a problem. She changed her tactics.

'Okay, who is in charge around here? Who was chosen to be captain of this ship? Who makes the decisions?' she said.

All the pirates turned and pointed at her. They knew when they were beaten.

'Good,' said the little girl, 'then that's decided and *everyone* is happy.'

'Really,' she thought, 'pirates are so gullible.'

4 'School Ahoy!'

On Monday morning, as the sun began to rise, *The Flying Dragon* left the open sea and sailed into the mouth of the wide river. Soon it reached the fork where the river joined the canal. It glided along the canal until, at last, the school came into view.

'School ahoy!' called the little girl. 'Weigh anchor, lads.'

The pirates lowered the gang-plank and left the ship. They crept across the playing-field and entered the school porch. The little girl pushed

the front door open and they all peered inside. It was about 11 o'clock. The children had just returned from morning break and the school was very quiet. Every sound seemed to echo down the tiled corridor.

The little girl felt nervous to be coming into school at this time. It was like having been to the dentist and coming back late, feeling strange and shy. But she found herself carried along by the others. They just wanted to get it over with and get back to the ship. They felt uncomfortable on dry land.

In front of the hall a display of dinosaur models was gathering dust. Footprints in powder paint led all the way into the boys' cloakroom.

'What a fine mess,' said Jethro. 'Doesn't anyone keep this place clean?'

While the others were arguing in which direction to go, he took off his scarf and began to polish the brass handles on the hall door.

'Oh dear, stewed cabbage and burnt rice pudding, I should guess,' said Joshua. He followed a terrible smell which drifted along the corridor from the school kitchen. Peeping through an open classroom door, Jem could see a sewing group waiting patiently while someone's mum threaded needles for a long line of children. He thought he would go in and give her a hand.

By the time the little girl and Jake entered the secretary's office they had lost the rest of the gang. Miss Crow, the school secretary, was arranging an enormous heap of money into tidy piles and scribbling sums on the edge of her blotting-pad. She looked tired and irritable. She kept sighing and scratching her head.

They waited for her to look up from her sums but she didn't. Finally she spoke, 'Put it down on the table,' and then, 'thank you!'

When Jake moved forward at the sight of so much money, she snapped, 'Keep those fat little fingers off my money.' He jumped back in alarm, looking guiltily at his hands.

The little girl decided to take over, 'We've come for the money,' she said. Miss Crow was not impressed. She still didn't look up.

'Well, it isn't ready yet,' she said. 'And don't

use that tone with me. Really, I've only one pair of hands, you know. It's always the same on a Monday. Rush, rush, rush. I do the best I can and if it isn't good enough . . . well . . . I'm sorry but . . .'

The little girl and Jake backed out of the secretary's office and closed the door quietly. They both felt guilty.

'Curdled custard!' whispered Jake, and the little girl nodded in agreement.

At that moment they heard a voice coming from the hall, which the little girl recognised. It was the voice of Mrs Raven, the headmistress. She didn't sound at all happy either.

'No, no, no, that's hopeless,' she said in a weary voice. 'You're supposed to be fierce and bloodthirsty. You wouldn't frighten a rice-pudding. If only we had some real pirates,' she said, 'then we might see some action.'

At this, the little girl and Jake began to feel better. They drew their pirate pistols and rushed into the hall.

'Abandon ship, you miserable varmints, or we'll string you from the flag-pole,' roared the little girl. Children flew screaming in all directions. Some of them hid behind Mrs Raven.

The little girl looked at them. They were children she knew and they were all wearing pirate outfits. She felt cheated. She stared open-mouthed at them while they stared back at her. It wasn't fair. She was speechless.

But Mrs Raven was delighted. 'Oh, well done, Mary Mansfield! That's more like it. We must find a part for you in our play.' The children were crowding around her and Mrs Raven was patting her on the back.

'That's what I wanted, children, a really bold pirate voice. You've got to sound like pirates, as well as looking like them. Your ... er ... friend looks the part,' she said politely, turning to Jake. 'Perhaps you might be able to advise us on costume, Mr ... ?'

'Jake Juggins, at your service, your honour,' said Jake, shaking hands roughly with the headmistress. Seeing the little girl busy with her friends, he added, '*Captain* of *The Flying Dragon*.'

Mrs Raven sent the children back to their classrooms. Then she explained to Jake that they were practising for the Christmas play. They were doing *Peter Pan*. Mrs Raven told Jake she was having problems with the pirates. Jake gave her lots of advice. He told her what the pirates should wear and the kinds of things they should say. A few of these ideas were not quite suitable, but Mrs Raven was far too tactful to say so.

At dinnertime the little girl went to look for the pirates. She found Joshua in the school kitchen, helping to serve the dinners. Jethro was telling the school caretaker how to get a better shine on the hall floor. Jem was teaching two young boys to sew buttons back on their coats. They'd been having a fight in the playground.

Peeping through the office window, she spotted Jake, who was now having a cup of tea with the headmistress. Mrs Raven had a selection of maps and a huge globe. There were countries marked that Jake had never even heard of.

'Great Goulash, your worship,' said Jake, who had never met a headmistress before, 'you run a splendid ship, if I may make so bold.'

As for Mary Mansfield, she was happy to be back. She became the heroine of the school. She was glad she hadn't missed the play. She was bound to get the part of Captain Hook. All her friends wanted to hear about her adventures. She told them how she captured a band of cut-throat pirates single-handed, became their captain, led raids on enemy ships and collected enough treasure to sink a school. At last, when she got tired of the life, she had tricked the pirates into bringing her home. And to prove it — here she was.

She discovered that telling the stories was nearly as good as having the adventures. She thought she might be a writer when she grew up. She already had lots of ideas. She was, after all, a very clever little girl. But then, most girls are, in my experience.

I am the genie of the bottle

The Not-So-Clever Genie

5 Mary Meets the Genie

One day, not long after her adventure with the pirates, Mary Mansfield was walking home from school across the playing fields. She was thinking that in most of her favourite stories it was the boys who had the best adventures. Now, Mary couldn't understand why this should be. After all, she knew that girls are just as brave as boys and equally as clever. If she could only find an adventure of her own, she could prove it.

She kicked a stone which flew up in the air. When it landed there was a loud chinking sound. Hidden in the long grass was a dusty old bottle. Mary was curious so she opened it and peered inside. It had a musty smell which made her cough. She quickly held the bottle away from her, which was a good thing in the circumstances.

Out of it poured a stream of evil-smelling smoke which swirled around her, hissing nastily. Then, before her eyes, it took on the shape of an enormous man, wearing ear-rings and a turban. In a booming voice he said,

'I am the Genie of the Bottle. What is your wish, O mistress?'

Well, Mary knew all about genies. She knew you had to be careful not to waste wishes. You might only get three. You might only get one. You might easily wish yourself into a lot of trouble. So she was quiet for a moment while she gave it some thought.

The genie towered over her, his arms folded. When she didn't answer he looked down in disgust. Mary could tell by his face that this genie had a very high opinion of himself and a very low opinion of little girls.

What is your wish O mistress?

'Tell me, O mistress, what is your wish? Command and I must obey. But please ... decide quickly.'

Mary Mansfield didn't like to be rushed. It wasn't every day that you were granted your dearest wish. She was determined to make the most of it. 'How many wishes do I get?' she asked.

'Three,' sighed the genie. He could see this was going to take all day.

At last Mary decided on her first wish. She said, 'I would like to be a knight in shining armour at the Court of King Arthur.' The genie threw back his head and roared with laughter.

'Out of the question, O microscopic one. A most unsuitable wish for such a very little girl,' he said, 'in my humble opinion.'

'No one asked for your opinion,' said Mary. She wasn't going to be bossed around by a genie.

'Isn't it true,' she asked, 'that whoever frees you from the bottle is your master?'

'This is true, O *mistress*.'

'And isn't it true that whatever your *mistress* desires you must do?'

'This is also true, O ingenious one. I fear this is true.'

'Then *you* will have to do as *I* say, won't you?' And she pointed a small, but determined, finger at the genie.

'Very well, O cunning one. Your wish is my command.' And the genie raised his hands and gave three thundering claps.

The ground began to tremble; the air seemed to vibrate. Mary had the feeling that she was travelling down a long tunnel. She smiled to herself. She had told that bossy genie a thing or two. She would keep him in his place.

'After all,' she thought, 'my wish is his command and he'd better not forget it.' The genie also smiled. He was planning to show her a thing or two.

'Fear not, O pocket-sized one,' he muttered, 'I will grant your wish, *in my own way*. After all, little *girls* should be kept in their proper place, in my *most* humble opinion.'

6 Mary's First Wish

When Mary opened her eyes, she found herself in a small clearing on the edge of a forest. Above the treetops she could see the towers of a great castle. It certainly looked as if the genie had got it right. But then she noticed her clothes. She was dressed in a long pink gown and satin slippers. And what's more, she was tied to a tree!

'That rotten genie,' she cried. 'I bet this was his stupid idea. A princess! I wouldn't put it past him to have left me here as a dragon's dinner.' And that was just what the genie had done. Across the clearing a large dragon sat staring at her, making low growling noises deep in his stomach.

'Ughhh, not another one,' he moaned. He laid his head on the ground and sighed.

Mary knew that she ought to feel afraid of the dragon. But he didn't look frightening, he looked utterly miserable.

'What's the matter?' she asked.

'Indigestion,' said the dragon. 'Last night's supper seems to have upset me.' Mary wasn't sure she wanted to know what the dragon had eaten for supper, but he told her.

'A rather old princess and half a knight is very heavy on the stomach, you know.' And he burped politely behind his paw.

'It serves you right, if you ask me,' said Mary. 'You shouldn't go around eating people.'

'But that's what dragons are supposed to eat,' he said crossly. 'Don't you know anything?'

'I know I wouldn't go on eating something if it gave me stomachache,' she said. 'My mum says you should rest your stomach if it hurts.'

'I suppose that might help,' said the dragon. 'Perhaps I will have a short nap. Now, don't go away. I might be hungry when I wake up.' And he fell asleep.

A moment later a knight on horseback appeared. He wore a suit of shining armour and carried a magnificent sword.

'That should have been me,' thought Mary. When the knight saw her he rode forward. But when he spotted the dragon he turned, as if to ride off.

'Hey!' called Mary. 'What about me?'

'Shshsh,' whispered the knight. 'You'll wake the dragon.'

'But you can't leave me here,' said Mary.

'Why not?' said the knight. 'Give me one good reason.'

'Because he'll eat me,' said Mary. 'And anyway I thought knights were supposed to be brave and bold.'

'Well, I'm not brave,' said the knight, 'I never have been. I don't see why people expect all knights to be brave.' And he blew his nose hard.

Mary felt sorry for him. She didn't like the way people expected all little girls to be sweet and quiet either. After all, most of them aren't.

'Look,' said Mary, 'don't worry. You untie me and lend me your sword and armour and I'll fight the dragon instead.'

'Won't you be afraid?' asked the knight.

'No,' said Mary, 'not at all.'

'I think I should have been born a princess,' he said. 'I'd have been a lot happier.'

The knight hid nervously behind the tree while Mary put on his armour. She picked up the magnificent sword.

'I'd love my friends to see me now,' she shouted. Suddenly there was a great rumble of thunder. Every tree in the forest shook. She had woken the dragon.

'Oh no, help!' cried the knight. 'Run for your life!' But Mary did no such thing. This was the chance she had been looking for. She pointed the heavy sword at the dragon.

'Prepare to meet your fate,' she said. The huge beast rose up from the ground, breathing flames of fire at her. The knight covered his eyes; he couldn't bear to watch. But Mary wasn't afraid.

'If that rotten genie could see me now,' she thought, 'I'd show him what little girls are really made of.' She took two steps towards the dragon, which gave a mighty roar, 'Hhraaaargh!'

Just then a whirlwind whipped across the clearing. In it Mary could see the grinning face of the genie. He swept her up in his arms and carried her back along the tunnel. She landed safe and sound, but absolutely furious, on the playing field.

'Snatched from the jaws of death,' said the genie. Mary opened her mouth to speak.

'Do not thank me, O mistress. I am but your humble genie.'

Mary spluttered, 'Thank you! But you ruined everything.'

'O ungrateful girl, O thankless thimbleful, it is my unhappy fate to protect . . .' grumbled the genie.

'I don't need you to protect me,' said Mary. 'All I want is some real excitement.'

The genie sighed. 'O almost invisible one, what is your second wish?'

Mary thought hard. She must choose carefully this time. She had always wanted to join a circus. Surely the genie couldn't mess that up.

'For my second wish I would like to perform in a circus ...' she began. At once the genie clapped his hands and carried her away.

'This time I will provide some real excitement,' said the genie. And his laughter echoed along the tunnel.

'Now what's he up to?' thought Mary.

7 Mary's Second Wish

The moment Mary's feet touched the ground she could hear the circus band. She could smell the sawdust and the animals.

'This time,' she thought, 'the genie must have got it right.' But when she looked down she wasn't so sure. She was wearing a leotard and tights, which was okay, but she was tied up again. Hundreds of eyes were fixed on her.

Facing her was a fierce man dressed as a Red Indian and called Little Hawk. In his hand he had a sharp knife. Mary didn't like the way he seemed to be pointing it in her direction. She closed her eyes just in time. WHAM! A knife whistled past her ear. WHAM! Then another. WHAM! WHAM! WHAM! The knives flew around her. The last one trimmed her hair on top. Mary wondered how she would explain that to her mum.

Little Hawk smiled and bowed. Mary would have liked to take a bow. After all, she had done the dangerous part. But Little Hawk pushed her out of the ring and said,

'Why you move, foolish girl! Next time you move ... CKCKCK!' And he drew a nasty finger down his ear. Mary didn't like that Little Hawk. She didn't want to be in his act. She wanted to be the one *throwing* the knives.

'Hurry up. You're on next,' called a circus boy. He gave Mary a crash helmet and pushed her back into the ring. Mary was surprised to see Little Hawk there again, wearing a flying-suit. This time he was called The Wonderful Waldo. He pointed to a set of ladders.

'Climb up,' he whispered. 'We're ready to fire.' At the top Mary found herself looking down the barrel of a huge gun.

'You're not firing me,' she said. But he pushed her in.

'And now . . . Ladies and Gentlemen . . . I, The Wonderful Waldo, will fire my very own invention, The Human Cannon. It will shoot Mary, our human cannonball, through the air, where she will make a death-defying leap into a tank of shark-infested water!'

'Sharks!' said Mary Mansfield. 'Oh no I won't.' But it was too late. There was a loud drum roll. Then . . .

'5–4–3–2–1 . . . Blast Off!' said The Wonderful Waldo.

Mary flew over the ring. She turned three times in the air and dropped into the tank.

Down, down, down she went until her feet touched the bottom. Then glug, glug, glug she rose to the surface. Three grinning sharks followed her up. But the circus boy fished her out, just in time. The Wonderful Waldo smiled and bowed. Mary would have liked to take a bow. After all, she had done the dangerous part. But he pushed her out of the ring.

'You were supposed to dive head-first into the water, foolish girl,' he said. 'Next time I intend to fire you straight through the roof, all the way to the moon!' Mary didn't like that Wonderful Waldo. She didn't want to be in his act. She wanted to be the one *firing* the cannon.

'Hurry up. You're on next,' called the circus boy. He gave her a new leotard, covered with sequins and feathers.

'What do I have to do this time?' asked Mary.

'The famous Italian magician, The Marvellous Mario, is going to saw you in half,' he told her.

'Oh no he's not,' thought Mary Mansfield. In the middle of the ring was The Marvellous Mario. Mary thought she had seen him somewhere before.

'Quickly! Quickly! I am waiting,' he whispered. Then he smiled at the crowd, as if everything was fine. He held up three brass rings. He did a trick where he joined the rings together. He gave Mary the rings to hold.

'I bet I could do that trick,' thought Mary.

Next he put a silk scarf over a tall black hat. He pulled out a real rabbit. He gave Mary the rabbit to hold.

'I'd like to do that trick,' thought Mary, stroking the rabbit's fur.

'Put it down. I am waiting,' the magician snarled. Then he smiled again, as if everything was fine.

'And now ... Ladies and Gentlemen ... of all the tricks, the most difficult. I cut this little girl in half but I do not harm even a hair of her pretty little head.'

'That's what you think,' said Mary Mansfield.

The magician pointed to a large wooden box.

'Get inside,' he hissed. 'Quickly!'

'No,' said Mary.

'But why?' he whispered.

'I'm frightened of mice,' said Mary.

'Mice?' said the magician. 'But there are no mice in the box.'

'Prove it,' said Mary.

'But how?' The Marvellous Mario was almost in tears.

'You get in the box first,' said Mary, 'then I'll know it's safe.'

'What's going on?' muttered the audience.

'Okay,' announced the magician. 'First I prove that the box is completely empty.' And he added under his breath, 'And that there are no mice in the box.' The Marvellous Mario climbed in. He lay there.

'The box is completely empty . . .' he said.

'Completely empty,' repeated Mary Mansfield. She slammed the lid down. She fastened the locks. She picked up the enormous steel saw. It looked like half a crocodile's mouth.

'And now . . . Ladies and Gentlemen . . . the most difficult trick of all . . . I shall cut this hopeless magician in half without harming a single hair of his big bald head.'

The audience clapped and cheered. The drums rolled. Mary began to saw. Zzzzzz . . . once . . . Zzzzzz . . . twice. The sawdust fell to the floor. Mary smiled. She didn't need that useless genie. She could manage all on her own.

'Let me out!' called The Marvellous Mario.

But Mary did no such thing. She drove the saw deeper . . . and deeper . . . Zzzzzzz. She would have loved the genie to see her now.

All of a sudden a strong wind swept through the big top and carried her up, up into the air.

'Oh no, not again,' thought Mary.

8 Mary's Third Wish

Mary Mansfield landed with a bump on the school field. By now the sky was beginning to turn dark. Mary was getting tired of the genie. He looked pretty cross with her too.

'For my third wish . . .' she said. The genie groaned.

'It was my hope, O obstinate one, that you might have had enough excitement for one day.' But Mary wasn't going to give up that easily.

'For my third wish,' she began again, 'I would like to be an astronaut.'

Well, this time the genie didn't say it was an unsuitable wish for a little girl. In fact he didn't say anything, because he didn't have the slightest idea what an astronaut was. He didn't want to admit that, so he kept quiet hoping she would give him a clue.

'Go on,' said Mary. 'Turn me into an astronaut. I want to fly through space ... Wheeeeeeee!'

'Ah,' thought the genie, 'this must be some strange modern name for a magic carpet.' That was easy to arrange. He would take her for a short trip around the field then, at last, he would be rid of her.

'Your wish is my command,' said the genie. He raised his hands and clapped three times.

What's this for?

Mary shivered. She was really cold and no wonder. When she looked down she wasn't wearing a space-suit; she was dressed in a pair of fine, baggy pants and a little veil. On the floor at her feet lay a scruffy piece of carpet.

'What's this for?' asked Mary.

'You wished to travel through space, did you not?' said the genie. 'Please step on and then we can begin.'

'I don't believe it,' thought Mary. 'This genie couldn't magic his way out of a paper bag, in my humble opinion.' She hesitated but she could see that the genie wouldn't wait. She stepped on and away they went.

First they flew smoothly through the air. They circled over the school roof. Dozens of lost tennis balls filled the gutters. Mary would have liked to stop and collect them, but the carpet moved on. It sailed over the library and the health centre.

'Can we go a bit faster?' she asked.

'If it is your wish,' sighed the genie.

Soon they were travelling at speed. Mary held onto a corner of the carpet. She would have loved her friends to see her now. She would have waved to them.

'This is great!' she said.

The genie was surprised. 'We strive to please,' he said. He was glad that she was happy, but by now he wasn't feeling very happy himself.

'You look a funny colour,' said Mary. 'Are you all right?' The genie groaned. He had been flying magic carpets for thousands of years but he still got travel sick. He couldn't wait for this trip to be over.

'I don't mind if you want to get off,' said Mary.

'You are so kind,' said the genie. But he didn't trust Mary Mansfield. He thought she was too

clever by half. If he got off now he might never see his carpet again. They began to argue. The genie didn't notice the church tower. Mary noticed, but it was too late.

'Look out!' she cried, as they skimmed over it.

The weather vane hooked Mary by the seat of her pants. She hung there, blowing in the wind, pointing east. The genie and the magic carpet had completely disappeared. She was all on her own and for the first time she was in real danger. Wherever was that useless genie now that she needed him? Nowhere to be seen.

Well, it was lucky for Mary Mansfield that the church tower was being repaired. There was scaffolding on all sides of it, all the way to the ground.

If she could first free herself from the weather-vane, she might be able to climb down. But there was no way of cutting herself loose so there was only one thing she could do. Holding tight to the top of the tower she slid out of her baggy pants and left them hanging there like a flag. She was glad it was nearly dark as she climbed down. She didn't want any of her friends to see her in her knickers.

Mary was furious when she reached the ground to see the genie leaning against a gravestone.

'Where were you when I was in danger?' she asked.

'Your three wishes are over, O troublesome one. I am now free of your command. And, as you have told me before, you can look after yourself.' Mary was really angry.

'You are the most useless genie in the world,' she told him.

'Take care,' warned the genie, 'that you do not make me angry, O reckless one.' But Mary wasn't afraid of him. She was planning to teach him a lesson. In his hand the genie still carried the dusty old bottle.

'If you are so clever,' said Mary, 'prove it. Show me how an enormous genie like you can fit into that little bottle.' Now, the genie didn't like to be called useless. And he could never resist a chance to show off. He drew himself up to his full height, then turned into a stream of smoke.

It whirled around Mary's head then shot into the bottle, disappearing from sight. Mary smiled as she screwed the bottle tight. It was the oldest trick of all and he had fallen for it. Mary knew it because she'd read 'Tales of the Arabian Nights', but the genie hadn't.

'That should put a stop to his tricks,' she thought, as she made her way across the field to collect her schoolbag.

Mary changed into her P.E. kit. Then she tore a piece of paper from her notebook and wrote on it, 'Handle this bottle with care. This genie is not to be trusted.' She stuck it on and walked to the edge of the field and onto the canal bank. She threw the bottle into the water and watched as it bobbed away down the canal.

By now it was really dark. Mary set off home. She wondered what she would tell her mum about her unexpected haircut. Well, she would think of something. There wasn't much Mary Mansfield couldn't do, if she set her mind to it.

'Who needs a genie anyway?' she thought. 'Girls can make their own adventures. It only takes intelligence and a lot of imagination. And, after all, that's what little girls are made of, in my humble opinion.'

You Herman, Me Mary

9 Kidnapped!

One long, hot day in the summer holidays, Mary Mansfield walked along a winding path through a wood. She had her hands pushed deep into her pockets. These were full of pine cones and owl pellets and rubber bands and other useful things you might need on an adventure. Mary Mansfield was always on the lookout for adventure. So she was quite excited when she heard an unusual call coming through the trees.

'Ah-ah-ah-ah-ah-ahhhhhh.'

Mary looked up into the branches above her head. Suddenly a big, strong man came sailing through the air on the end of a long grass rope. He wore a leopard skin and was followed by a monkey. They landed at Mary's feet. The man beat his chest a couple of times and then said, in a deep voice,

'Me Herman, King of the Jungle.'

'Me Mary,' said Mary. 'What happened to Tarzan?'

'Him retired. Now Herman in charge.'

'Ugh-ugh agh-agh ugh-ugh,' said the monkey.

'Him Chumley,' said Herman.

Mary smiled at the monkey and politely held out her hand. But the monkey was busy jabbing a long brown finger at her, then jumping up in the air and turning somersaults in his excitement.

'Ugh-ugh-ugh ugh-ugh-ugh-ugh,' he said. And he kept on pointing.

Mary wanted to tell the monkey it was rude to point at people. It was rude to stare too. They were both staring at her. Then Herman began to shake his head, but the monkey wouldn't take no for an answer.

'Eegh eegh eegh eegh eegh,' he insisted.

Herman sighed and said, 'Chumley him say, "Can Girl read?"'

'Yes,' said Mary. She was quite a good reader. The monkey clapped his hands and chattered some more.

Herman asked, 'Him say, "Can Girl read *long words?*"'

'Mmmm, yes,' said Mary, 'quite long words.'

Herman didn't look as if he believed her, she was such a little girl. 'But can Girl read *joined writing?*' He was sure this time he would catch her out.

'Well, it depends on the writing,' said Mary. 'I can read my mum's and my dad can't.'

Herman was still doubtful, but the monkey looked as if he'd just won a bet.

'Hee-hee-hee-hee,' he said.

'Girl come with Herman,' said Herman crossly. 'Herman have job for Girl.'

'What kind of job?' she asked suspiciously. And she backed away.

Mary had almost been caught like this before by a gang of pirates. She didn't want to end up cooking and cleaning for this strongman and a bad-tempered monkey.

'What kind of job?' she asked again.

'Girl soon find out,' said Herman. He leaned forward, picked up Mary and bundled her under his arm. Before she could speak he broke into a run. Then he leapt into the air and swung off, back through the woods, calling, 'Ahhh ah-ah-ah-ah-ah-ahhhhhh.'

The monkey chattered and clapped his hands and did a little dance.

'Ugh-ugh-*ugh*,' he said, pretending to tuck something under his arm too. Then he grabbed a low-hanging branch and set off after them.

The monkey felt very pleased with himself. It was lucky that he was there to do Herman's thinking for him. If only humans had the brains of monkeys, he thought, how much cleverer they would be.

10 Back to the Jungle

Mary enjoyed the feeling of flying through the treetops. As the air rushed past her ears, she could see the trees changing by the minute. Soon the wood began to look more like a jungle. In a kind of blur, instead of sparrows and squirrels, she could make out parrots and monkeys. It was much hotter here, quite steamy, and the colours were brighter and richer.

Mary had never been in a jungle before. This was turning into an adventure after all, she thought.

When they got back to Herman's tree-house he looked around unhappily. Chumley seemed unhappy too. Mary looked at their long faces, then she looked at the untidy mess the place

was in. 'Oh no,' she thought. 'Who does the cleaning around here?' she asked. It seemed as if Jane had retired too.

'Wanda,' said Herman.

'Wanda?' said Mary.

Herman nodded. 'But Wanda gone.'

'What do you mean – gone?'

'Herman lose Wanda. Maybe Herman never see Wanda again,' he said.

'Huuuhhh huh-huh,' sobbed Chumley.

'But where has she gone?' asked Mary.

'How Herman know? This why Herman need Girl. Girl read Wanda's message.'

And he stuck a piece of bark under Mary's nose.

'Ugh-ugh, ugh-ugh,' said the monkey, jabbing at the message as if to hurry Mary.

'All right, all right,' said Mary. He was the most bad-mannered monkey she had ever met. Mary read out loud:

It's my birthday – felt like a complete change. Gone hunting. You two can get the tea. Love Wanda

'I don't blame her,' said Mary. 'I'd prefer hunting to cooking, especially on my birthday. You two had better get the tea.'

Herman grunted and so did the monkey. They thought Mary should mind her own business.

'Jungle not safe for Wanda,' said Herman. 'Maybe wild animals steal Wanda.'

'No,' said Mary. 'I bet she's having a good time. How long has she been gone?'

'Five days,' said Herman sadly.

'Five days!' said Mary. It did sound serious after all. What were they doing, wasting their time here? They should have been out finding Wanda.

'Well, come on,' she said. 'We'd better look for her.'

But Herman folded his arms. 'Girl stay home. Men find Wanda.'

'Eegh eegh eegh eegh,' said Chumley in total agreement.

Mary ignored the monkey. 'You might need my help,' she said.

At this the monkey fell over on the ground and rolled around laughing. Even Herman laughed.

'What can Girl do that man and ape cannot?'

Mary could think of lots of things.

'I'm the one that can read,' she reminded them. 'What if Wanda's left other messages, clues, that kind of thing, who'll read them?'

Herman was impressed by this argument. 'Very well, Girl come too.' And they set off along the track at a jog.

Chumley followed them, grumbling to himself. He wasn't very happy. He thought he would have to keep his eye on Mary. He could see that this little girl was used to getting her own way.

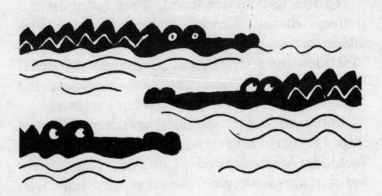

11 Crocodiles!

For some time they went on in silence, Herman leading the way. They headed for the river, a favourite hunting place.

'First Herman find Wanda's tracks. Then follow Wanda's trail.'

'I'm good at tracking and stalking,' said Mary. She'd just learnt it in the Guides.

'Err err errrr,' said the monkey rudely. He was getting fed up with all the things Mary Mansfield could do.

When they came to the river they saw human footprints in the mud. And lots of animal prints too, all criss-crossing each other, leading off in every direction.

Herman was more worried now. Especially when he noticed that the human prints led down to the water's edge and then disappeared.

'Crocodiles!' he growled. They were an old
enemy of his. 'Crocodiles steal Wanda. Why
Herman not think of that?'

And without a moment's hesitation he dived
into the water and swam fast against the
current, carrying a knife between his teeth.

Mary and the monkey watched Herman
disappear round a bend in the river.

'Come on,' shouted Mary, breaking into a
run. The monkey tried to keep up with her,
chattering at her to wait for him.

When they turned the bend they could see Herman again in the middle of the river. They could see the banks of the river, thick with crocodiles.

In minutes a dozen eased themselves out of the mud and headed in Herman's direction, their mouths snapped open in readiness. Mary could see their teeth shining like rows of little daggers.

'Look out!' she cried.

As the first swam closer Herman was prepared, knife in hand, to meet it. Wrapping his huge arm round the crocodile's jaws, he forced them closed. Then he trod water while he struggled with the crocodile's long snout under his arm. Herman lifted his knife, but before he could use it, Mary again called, 'Look out! There's one behind you.'

Whichever way Herman turned he looked down the throat of a hungry crocodile.

Mary shook her head. She thought, 'I bet Tarzan looked before *he* jumped.'

The monkey was shrieking at her to do something.

'You do something,' she said. So the monkey put his hands over his eyes and hid his head.

She could see it was up to her to save Herman. She dug deep into her pocket and pulled out a handful of thick rubber bands. Clutching them, Mary dived into the river and swam fast towards him.

Herman was busy trying to beat off two other crocodiles while he struggled with the first one. Mary stretched a rubber band and slipped it over the crocodile's snout. The furious beast lashed the water with its tail. As fast as Herman could grab another, Mary fixed its jaws together. Soon they were all well and truly gagged. With no other means of attack they floated off in disgust.

When Herman and Mary climbed out onto the river-bank, Herman looked very pleased with himself. He beat his chest and roared,

'Herman teach crocodiles big lesson. Herman – King of the Jungle. And crocodiles better not forget it.'

Chumley clapped and chattered in praise of Herman.

'Ugh-ugh-ugh Agh-agh-agh Ow-ow-ow,' he flattered him. The two of them went back into the jungle, arms round each other, like two heroes.

Mary watched them go.

'King of the Jungle!' she thought. It was lucky that she'd been there or Herman might have ended up on the crocodiles' next menu. 'And serve him right,' she thought, 'if he had.'

12 Snakes!

When Mary caught up with them, she found them sitting on the ground, discussing Herman's 'single-handed' victory. They had completely forgotten about her. They had forgotten about Wanda too.

'Well,' said Mary, 'now we know the crocodiles don't have her.'

Herman jumped up and headed off in one bound. 'This time follow jungle path.'

'Wait for us,' called Mary. She and the monkey tried to keep up but Herman raced on alone. Mary hoped he wouldn't rush into any more reckless situations. But too late, he already had.

Herman suddenly came to a sandy hollow where hundreds of snakes lay sunning themselves. One large, thoughtless python lay right across the path and Herman tripped over it. He fell headlong and lay for a moment stunned.

Within seconds the snakes slithered towards him.

'Ssssuch a ssssurprissse,' they hissed. 'Sssso unexxxpected.'

Although these were not poisonous snakes, they were still deadly. They coiled their long bodies around Herman and squeezed him tight, until he could hardly breathe.

Mary and the monkey arrived as Herman tried to sit up and free himself. But he was tied, hand and foot. He strained every muscle until one hand was free. Then he peeled the snakes off, one after another, and threw them aside.

As fast as he did this the slippery creatures slid back and started to tie him up again.

Mary turned to the monkey for help. But Chumley hated snakes even more than crocodiles. 'Ow-ow-ow-ow-ow,' he cried.

Mary couldn't decide who was more trouble, Herman or the monkey. Fortunately just then she had one of her good ideas. She had recently done a Guide badge on knots. She rushed forward and caught the next two snakes which Herman tossed aside. She quickly turned them into a tight reef knot.

'Left over right, through and over. Right over left, through and – pull.'

'Ssssstop that,' said the snakes.

But Mary threw the snakes into the trees where they lay studying their tails, wondering how they would ever get free.

She turned to the next snake and tied a 'running bowline' knot.

'Loop first, then the rabbit comes out of the hole,' she reminded herself, 'round the tree and down the hole again. Then pull it . . . tight.'

'Ssssspare usss,' hissed the snake. But Mary went on to do a few more of these before moving on to her favourite knot.

Using a nearby branch to tie them to, she did a whole row of clove hitches. The surprised snakes resembled a line of washing, hanging out to dry.

She tied another dozen in pairs, this time using a fisherman's knot. The snakes hissed at one another as they tried to untie themselves.

Next she did some figure of eights, a donkey hitch, a sheepshank and finished off with a double sheet bend.

Herman glanced around him with real pleasure and dusted himself off. He said, 'Let this be a lesson. Never tangle with Herman, King of the Jungle, or snakes will be sorry.'

'Ssssorry,' said one sad snake. 'You can ssssay that again.'

The monkey picked up one or two twisted shapes and threw them like hoops to Herman. It soon turned into quite a game.

Mary shook her head. She could see they'd completely forgotten Wanda again. It was lucky she was there to remind them.

'Well,' she said. 'Now we know the snakes don't have her.'

13 Queen of the Apes

Herman looked unhappy; he had no ideas left.

'What we need is a plan,' said Mary. 'Surely if Wanda is here in the jungle there must be some creature who knows where she is.'

Herman and Chumley scratched their heads, as if Mary had asked them a very difficult riddle.

'Perhaps one of the birds,' she suggested.

Herman's face lit up. Why hadn't he thought of that?

He gave a long whistle, then called, 'Ahhh ah-ah-ah-ah-ah-ahhhhhh.'

Soon the air above them was filled with the beating of a large bird's wings. A brightly-coloured parrot flew into the trees and perched there, fluffing its feathers.

'Herman search for Wanda. Maybe parrot see Wanda?'

'Caws,' said the parrot. 'Seen her with the apes. Sent you a message.'

The parrot uncurled its claw and flew off. Something fell to the ground. Herman and Chumley pretended to read it, but neither of them could. They passed it to Mary. She could see it was Wanda's writing.

'It's an invitation. It says, Barbecue Party. Everybody welcome. Bring a Banana. It's signed – Wanda of the Apes.'

'Apes!' growled Herman.

The apes had always been jealous of him. Now they had stolen Wanda. Well they wouldn't get away with it.

Off Herman went, swinging through the trees. Mary and Chumley followed. When they reached the ape village they hid behind some bushes.

A grand feast was set out on plates made of large leaves. In the centre of a clearing a deep pit had been dug and filled with fire. It glowed red. Beside it were a number of long, pointed spears. It looked as if a horrible sacrifice was about to take place.

A number of monkeys and other animals sat round chattering excitedly. As they watched, four larger monkeys appeared, carrying a platform, on which was seated a small, fair-haired woman. Mary knew straight away this must be Wanda.

All the monkeys fell silent and turned to look at Wanda. They raised their coconuts, like people at a cocktail party. Wanda smiled and blushed.

Mary whispered to Herman, 'I think they're going to toast Wanda.'

Herman looked at the long spears and the glowing fire.

'No one toast Wanda,' he shouted. He leapt into the open with a terrifying yell, 'Ahhh ah-ah-ah-ah-ah-ahhhhhh!' scattering monkeys in all directions.

Soon the place was in panic. A few of the braver monkeys threw themselves onto

Herman. He spun round and round, swinging the monkeys off into the trees like a fairground ride out of control.

Mary could see that Wanda was trying to make herself heard over the noise, but her voice just disappeared. It was worse than the school playground. And that's what gave Mary the idea. Digging into her pocket she pulled out her Guide whistle. She put it to her mouth and gave three long blasts. The noise was deafening.

In a moment everyone went quiet. All the monkeys covered their ears and rolled their eyes. Even Herman went silent. Wanda looked around in surprise but when Mary stepped out she started to laugh.

Soon the curious monkeys crowded around Mary, wanting to blow on the magic whistle. They were so impressed by it they would gladly have made Mary Queen of the Apes too. Then Wanda took charge, 'No more fuss. Just sit down and we can carry on with the party.'

Immediately all the monkeys bowed and nodded and did as they were told.

'I'm the queen here now, you know,' she told Herman.

'Monkeys not steal Wanda?' he asked, surprised.

'Of course not. I got lost while I was hunting, then I found the monkeys. I like it here. I've set up a school,' she said proudly. 'I'm teaching them to cook. One or two are learning to read.'

'What about us?' asked Herman.

'Us-us-us-us-us?' echoed Chumley.

Wanda looked at them for a minute. 'Well, you can join us. But you'll have to work, like everyone else.'

'What about me?' asked Mary. She didn't think her mum would be keen on her living in an ape-village. And she had wanted to be home by tea-time, otherwise her dad would be out looking for her.

'Herman will take you back,' Wanda promised. 'But first you must try a barbecued banana. They are wonderful.' And she was right, they were.

When Mary left, everyone was sorry to see her go.

'Hmmm-hmmm-hmmm-hmmm,' said the monkey and gave her a kiss.

Mary gave Wanda the whistle, to keep the monkeys and Herman in order. She could buy a new one, before Guides started again.

Being a Girl Guide had been very useful on this adventure. She had certainly kept her Guide promise:

- To be prepared
- To think for herself
- And to cope with emergencies.

But then, most little girls are good at thinking for themselves, at least all the ones I know are, and believe me, I know a lot.

Annie Dalton

THE REAL TILLY BEANY

Matilda Beany, youngest of four, just does not want to be ordinary old Tilly Beany. Not all the time. There are too many other people she has to be. But when Tilly becomes the mysterious Windstar, Jellybear or Matilda Seaflower, it can be hard on the rest of the family. And when they find Cindertilly scrubbing the doorstep, things have really got out of hand . . .

Commended for the Carnegie Medal.

'a warm and delightful tale . . . Shortlisted for the 1991 Carnegie award, this book is one of the best to emerge for the younger age group for a long time.'

Gayner Eyre, *Junior Education*

'captures perfectly the world from the viewpoint of a small child . . .'

Weekend Telegraph

'This made us laugh out loud. A completely unpatronising book about a five-year-old with a huge imagination. Really refreshing.'

Carnegie Judges

A selected list of titles available from Mammoth

While every effort is made to keep prices low, it is sometimes necessary to increase prices at short notice. Mandarin Paperbacks reserves the right to show new retail prices on covers which may differ from those previously advertised in the text or elsewhere.

The prices shown below were correct at the time of going to press.

☐ 7497 0366 0	**Dilly the Dinosaur**	Tony Bradman	£2.50
☐ 7497 0137 4	**Flat Stanley**	Jeff Brown	£2.50
☐ 7497 0306 7	**The Chocolate Touch**	P Skene Catling	£2.50
☐ 7497 0568 X	**Dorrie and the Goblin**	Patricia Coombs	£2.50
☐ 7497 0114 5	**Dear Grumble**	W J Corbett	£2.50
☐ 7497 0054 8	**My Naughty Little Sister**	Dorothy Edwards	£2.50
☐ 7497 0723 2	**The Little Prince (colour ed.)**	A Saint-Exupery	£3.99
☐ 7497 0305 9	**Bill's New Frock**	Anne Fine	£2.99
☐ 7497 0590 6	**Wild Robert**	Diana Wynne Jones	£2.50
☐ 7497 0661 9	**The Six Bullerby Children**	Astrid Lindgren	£2.50
☐ 7497 0319 9	**Dr Monsoon Taggert's Amazing Finishing Academy**	Andrew Matthews	£2.50
☐ 7497 0420 9	**I Don't Want To!**	Bel Mooney	£2.50
☐ 7497 0833 6	**Melanie and the Night Animal**	Gillian Rubinstein	£2.50
☐ 7497 0264 8	**Akimbo and the Elephants**	A McCall Smith	£2.50
☐ 7497 0048 3	**Friends and Brothers**	Dick King-Smith	£2.50
☐ 7497 0795 X	**Owl Who Was Afraid of the Dark**	Jill Tomlinson	£2.99

All these books are available at your bookshop or newsagent, or can be ordered direct from the publisher. Just tick the titles you want and fill in the form below.

Mandarin Paperbacks, Cash Sales Department, PO Box 11, Falmouth, Cornwall TR10 9EN.

Please send cheque or postal order, no currency, for purchase price quoted and allow the following for postage and packing:

UK including BFPO £1.00 for the first book, 50p for the second and 30p for each additional book ordered to a maximum charge of £3.00.

Overseas including Eire £2 for the first book, £1.00 for the second and 50p for each additional book thereafter.

NAME (Block letters) ....

ADDRESS ....

....

☐ I enclose my remittance for ....

☐ I wish to pay by Access/Visa Card Number

Expiry Date